This Journal Belongs To:

_____

"Beyond the obvious facts that he has at some time done manual labour, that he takes snuff, that he is a Freemason, that he has been in China, and that he has done a considerable amount of writing lately, I can deduce nothing else."

Arthur Conan Doyle - The Adventures of Sherlock Holmes

Bookaful Press

As he stood by the desolate fire, he felt that the only one thing which could assuage his grief would be thorough and complete retribution, brought by his own hand upon his enemies.
- Arthur Conan Doyle: A Study in Scarlet

When a doctor does go wrong he is the first of criminals.
- Arthur Conan Doyle: The Adventure of the Speckled Band

I can never bring you to realise the importance of sleeves, the suggestiveness of thumb-nails, or the great issues that may hang from a boot-lace. - Arthur Conan Doyle: A Case of Identity

Give me your details, and from an armchair I will return you an
excellent expert opinion.
- Arthur Conan Doyle: The Adventure of Wisteria Lodge

It has long been an axiom of mine that the little things are infinitely the most important. - Arthur Conan Doyle: A Case of Identity

There is but one step from the grotesque to the horrible.
- Arthur Conan Doyle: The Adventure of Wisteria Lodge

Life is infinitely stranger than anything which the mind of man could invent. - Arthur Conan Doyle: A Case of Identity

As a rule, the more bizarre a thing is, the less mysterious it proves to be.
- Arthur Conan Doyle: The Adventures of Sherlock Holmes

My first glance is always at a woman's sleeve. In a man it is perhaps
better first to take the knee of the trouser.
- Arthur Conan Doyle: A Case of Identity

Draw your chair up, and hand me my violin, for the only problem which we have still to solve is how to while away these bleak autumnal evenings. - Arthur Conan Doyle: The Adventures of Sherlock Holmes

Never trust to general impressions, my boy, but concentrate yourself
upon details. - Arthur Conan Doyle: A Case of Identity

Sherlock Holmes was, as I expected, lounging about his sitting-room in
his dressing-gown, reading the agony column of The Times and
smoking his before-breakfast pipe.
- Arthur Conan Doyle: The Adventures of Sherlock Holmes

They are important, you understand, without being interesting.
- Arthur Conan Doyle: A Case of Identity

Singularity is almost invariably a clue.
- Arthur Conan Doyle: The Adventures of Sherlock Holmes

You see, but you do not observe.
- Arthur Conan Doyle: A Scandal in Bohemia

Take a pinch of snuff, doctor, and acknowledge that I have scored
over you in your example.
- Arthur Conan Doyle: The Adventures of Sherlock Holmes

'Dr. Watson, Mr. Sherlock Holmes,' said Stamford, introducing us.
- Arthur Conan Doyle: A Study in Scarlet

That which is clearly known hath less terror than that which is but hinted at and guessed. - Arthur Conan Doyle: The Adventures of Sherlock Holmes

From a drop of water," said the writer, "a logical man could understand oceans and waterfalls without having ever seen or heard of them. - Arthur Conan Doyle: A Study in Scarlet

The authorities are excellent at amassing facts, though they do not always use them to advantage.
- Arthur Conan Doyle: The Adventures of Sherlock Holmes

His Ignorance was as remarkable as his knowledge.
- Arthur Conan Doyle: A Study in Scarlet

The bent head, the averted eye, the faltering voice, the wincing figure-
these, and not the unshrinking gaze and frank reply, are the true signals
of passion. - Arthur Conan Doyle: The Adventures of Sherlock Holmes

It is not easy to express the inexpressible," he answered with a laugh.
- Arthur Conan Doyle: A Study in Scarlet

The emotional qualities are antagonistic to clear reasoning.
- Arthur Conan Doyle: The Adventures of Sherlock Holmes

It's quite exciting," said Sherlock Holmes, with a yawn.
- Arthur Conan Doyle: A Study in Scarlet

The plot thickens.
- Arthur Conan Doyle: The Adventures of Sherlock Holmes

London, that great cesspool into which all the loungers and idlers of the Empire are irresistibly drained. - Arthur Conan Doyle: A Study in Scarlet

The work is its own reward
- Arthur Conan Doyle: The Adventures of Sherlock Holmes

Patience, my friend, patience! You will find in time that it has everything to do with it. - Arthur Conan Doyle: A Study in Scarlet

The world is full of obvious things which nobody by any chance ever observes.
- Arthur Conan Doyle: The Adventures of Sherlock Holmes

Read it up — you really should. There is nothing new under the sun.
It has all been done before. - Arthur Conan Doyle: A Study in Scarlet

There are vague memories in our souls of those misty centuries when the world was in its childhood.- Arthur Conan Doyle: The Adventures of Sherlock Holmes

That hurts my pride, Watson. It is a petty feeling, no doubt, but it
hurts my pride. It becomes a personal matter with me now...
- Arthur Conan Doyle: A Study in Scarlet

They say that genius is an infinite capacity for taking pains.
- Arthur Conan Doyle: The Adventures of Sherlock Holmes

What you do in this world is a matter of no consequence,' returned my companion, bitterly. 'The question is, what can you make people believe that you have done?'
- Arthur Conan Doyle: A Study in Scarlet

This is not the time for humbugs, Watson!
- Arthur Conan Doyle: The Adventures of Sherlock Holmes

When a man writes on a wall, his instinct leads him to write above the level of his own eyes. - Arthur Conan Doyle: A Study in Scarlet

To underestimate oneself is as much an exaggeration of one's powers than the other. - Arthur Conan Doyle: The Adventures of Sherlock Holmes

It was easier to know it than to explain why I know it. If you were asked to prove that two and two made four, you might find some difficulty, and yet you are quite sure of the fact.
- Arthur Conan Doyle: A Study in Scarlet

Many men have been hanged on far slighter evidence,' I remarked. 'So they have. And many men have been wrongfully hanged.'
- Arthur Conan Doyle: The Boscombe Valley Mystery

There's the scarlet thread of murder running through the colorless skein of life, and our duty is to unravel it, and isolate it, and expose every inch of it. - Arthur Conan Doyle: A Study in Scarlet

There is nothing more deceptive than an obvious fact.
- Arthur Conan Doyle: The Boscombe Valley Mystery

It was easier to know it than to explain why I know it. If you were asked to prove that two and two made four, you might find some difficulty, and yet you are quite sure of the fact.
- Arthur Conan Doyle: A Study in Scarlet

It's every man's business to see justice done.
- Arthur Conan Doyle: The Crooked Man

When a fact appears to be opposed to a long train of deductions, it
invariably proves to be capable of bearing some other interpretation.
- Arthur Conan Doyle: A Study in Scarlet

It is stupidity rather than courage to refuse to recognize danger when it is close upon you. - Arthur Conan Doyle: The Final Problem

There is no branch of detective science which is so important and so
much neglected as the art of tracing footsteps.
- Arthur Conan Doyle: A Study in Scarlet

The man pervades London, and no one has heard of him. That's what puts him on a pinnacle in the records of crime.
- Arthur Conan Doyle: The Final Problem

All other men are specialists, but his specialism is omniscience.
- Arthur Conan Doyle: His Last Bow

You have probably never heard of Professor Moriarty?' said he.
'Never.' - Arthur Conan Doyle: The Final Problem

Good old Watson! You are the one fixed point in a changing age.
- Arthur Conan Doyle: His Last Bow

I have come for advice.' 'That is easily got.' 'And help.' 'That is not always so easy.' - Arthur Conan Doyle: The Five Orange Pips

He seems to have declared war on the King's English as well as on the English king. - Arthur Conan Doyle: His Last Bow

To the logician all things should be seen exactly as they are, and to underestimate one's self is as much a departure from truth as to exaggerate one's own powers. - Arthur Conan Doyle: The Greek interpreter

I follow my own methods, and tell as much or as little as I choose.
That is the advantage of being unofficial.
- Arthur Conan Doyle: Silver Blaze

A hound it was, an enormous coal-black hound, but not such a hound
as mortal eyes have ever seen.
- Arthur Conan Doyle: The Hound of the Baskervilles

It is more than possible; it is probable.
- Arthur Conan Doyle: Silver Blaze

For the one and only time I caught a glimpse of a great heart as well as of a great brain. - Arthur Conan Doyle: The Hound of the Baskervilles

What do you wish to draw my attention to? To the curious incident
of the dog in the night-time. The dog did nothing in the night-time.
That was the curious incident, remarked Sherlock Holmes.
- Arthur Conan Doyle: Silver Blaze

It is not what we know, but what we can prove
- Arthur Conan Doyle: The Hound of the Baskervilles

Have you tried to drive a harpoon through a body? No? Tut, tut, my
dear sir, you must really pay attention to these details.
- Arthur Conan Doyle: The Adventure of Black Peter

Some people without possesing genius have a remarkable power of stimulating it - Arthur Conan Doyle: The Hound of the Baskervilles

There can be no question, my dear Watson, of the value of exercise before breakfast. - Arthur Conan Doyle: The Adventure of Black Peter

You know, Watson, I don't mind confessing to you that I have always
had an idea that I would have made a highly efficient criminal.
- Arthur Conan Doyle: The Adventure of Charles Augustus Milverton

There is nothing more stimulating than a case where everything goes against you. - Arthur Conan Doyle: The Hound of the Baskervilles

I believe you are a wizard, Mr. Holmes.
- Arthur Conan Doyle: The Adventure of the Abbey Grange

His knowledge was greater than his wisdom, and his powers were far superior to his character. - Arthur Conan Doyle: The Leather Funnel

The game is afoot.
- Arthur Conan Doyle: The Adventure of the Abbey Grange

The charlatan is always the pioneer... The quack of yesterday is the professor of tomorrow. - Arthur Conan Doyle: The Leather Funnel

Holmes, you have an answer to everything
- Arthur Conan Doyle: The Adventure of the Blue Carbuncle

I confess that I have been as blind as a mole, but is is better to learn
wisdom late than never to learn it at all.
- Arthur Conan Doyle: The Man with the Twisted Lip

My name is Sherlock Holmes. It is my business to know what other people do not know.
- Arthur Conan Doyle: The Adventure of the Blue Carbuncle

You have a grand gift for silence, Watson. It makes you quite
invaluable as a companion.
- Arthur Conan Doyle: The Man with the Twisted Lip

Watson, you can see everything. You fail, however, to reason from
what you see.
- Arthur Conan Doyle: The Adventure of the Blue Carbuncle

It was difficult to refuse any of Sherlock Holmes' requests, for they were always so exceedingly definite, and put forward with such a quiet air of mastery.
- Arthur Conan Doyle: The Man with the Twisted Lip

How do you know that?' 'I followed you.' 'I saw no one.' 'That is what
you may expect to see when I follow you.'
- Arthur Conan Doyle: The Adventure of the Bruce-Partington Plans

Art in the blood is liable to take the strangest forms.
- Arthur Conan Doyle: The Memoirs of Sherlock Holmes

It was one of my friend's most obvious weaknesses that he was
impatient with less alert intelligences than his own.
- Arthur Conan Doyle: The Adventure of the Bruce-Partington Plans

Excellent!' I cried. 'Elementary,' said he.
- Arthur Conan Doyle: The Memoirs of Sherlock Holmes

When you have eliminated all which is impossible, then whatever
remains, however improbable, must be the truth.
- Arthur Conan Doyle: The Adventure of the Bruce-Partington Plans

for nothing clears up a case so much as stating it to another person.
- Arthur Conan Doyle: The Memoirs of Sherlock Holmes

Data! data! data!" he cried impatiently. "I can't make bricks without clay. - Arthur Conan Doyle: The Adventure of the Copper Beeches

Pray give my greetings to Mrs. Watson, and believe me to be, my dear
fellow, Very sincerely yours, SHERLOCK HOLMES.
- Arthur Conan Doyle: The Memoirs of Sherlock Holmes

It is my belief, Watson, founded upon my experience, that the lowest and vilest alleys in London do not present a more dreadful record of sin than does the smiling and beautiful countryside.
- Arthur Conan Doyle: The Adventure of the Copper Beeches

How are you, Watson?' said he, cordially. 'I should never have known you under that moustache' - Arthur Conan Doyle: The Naval Treaty

Every problem becomes very childish when once it is explained to you.
- Arthur Conan Doyle: The Adventure of the Dancing Men

It is quite a three pipe problem, and I beg that you won't speak to me for fifty minutes.
- Arthur Conan Doyle: The Red-Headed League

What one man can invent, another can discover.
- Arthur Conan Doyle: The Adventure of the Dancing Men

Before we begin to investigate that, let us try to realize what we do know, so as to make the most of it, and to separate the essential from the accidental.
- Arthur Conan Doyle: The Return of Sherlock Holmes

I fear that if the matter is beyond humanity, it is certainly beyond me.
- Arthur Conan Doyle: The Adventure of the Devil's Foot

By George!' cried the inspector. 'How did you ever see that?"Because I looked for it.' - Arthur Conan Doyle: The Return of Sherlock Holmes

The best way of successfully acting a part is to be it.
- Arthur Conan Doyle: The Adventure of the Dying Detective

Every man finds his limitations, Mr. Holmes, but at least it cures us
of the weakness of self-satisfaction.
- Arthur Conan Doyle: The Return of Sherlock Holmes

Work is the best antidote to sorrow, my dear Watson.
- Arthur Conan Doyle: The Adventure of the Empty House

Detection is, or ought to be, an exact science, and should be treated
in the same cold and unemotional manner.
- Arthur Conan Doyle: The Sign of Four

We were fairly accustomed to receive weird telegrams at Baker Street.
- Arthur Conan Doyle: The Adventure of the Golden Pince-Nez

I never make exceptions. An exception disproves the rule.
- Arthur Conan Doyle: The Sign of Four

We can't command our love, but we can our actions.
- Arthur Conan Doyle: The Adventure of the Noble Bachelor

It is of the first importance, not to allow your judgement to be
biased by personal qualities. A client is to me a mere unit, a factor in
a problem. - Arthur Conan Doyle: The Sign of Four

From the point of view of the criminal expert,' said Mr. Sherlock
Holmes, 'London has become a singularly uninteresting city since the
death of the late lamented Professor Moriarty.'
- Arthur Conan Doyle: The Adventure of the Norwood Builder

My mind rebels at stagnation, give me problems, give me work!
- Arthur Conan Doyle: The Sign of Four

I assure you, my good Lestrade, that I have an excellent reason for
everything that I do.
- Arthur Conan Doyle: The Adventure of the Norwood Builder

No, no: I never guess. It is a shocking habit—destructive to the
logical faculty. - Arthur Conan Doyle: The Sign of Four

Mr. Sherlock Holmes was leaning back in his chair after his whimsical
protest, and was unfolding his morning paper in a leisurely fashion,'
- Arthur Conan Doyle: The Adventure of the Norwood Builder

You have an extraordinary genius for minutiae
- Arthur Conan Doyle: The Sign of Four

You seem to have powers that are hardly human.
- Arthur Conan Doyle: The Adventure of the Priory School

You know my methods. Apply them.
- Arthur Conan Doyle: The Sign of Four

It is impossible as I state it, and therefore I must in some respect
have stated it wrong.
- Arthur Conan Doyle: The Adventure of the Priory School

Which is it to-day,' I asked, 'morphine or cocaine?'He raised his eyes
languidly from the old black-letter volume which he had opened.'It is
cocaine,' he said, 'a seven-per-cent solution. Would you care to try it?'
- Arthur Conan Doyle: The Sign of Four

What, indeed? It is art for art's sake, Watson.
- Arthur Conan Doyle: The Adventure of the Red Circle

He possesses two out of the three qualities necessary for the ideal detective. He has the power of observation and that of deduction. He is only wanting in knowledge. - Arthur Conan Doyle: The Sign of Four

It is a capital mistake to theorize before one has data. Insensibly one begins to twist facts to suit theories, instead of theories to suit facts.
- Arthur Conan Doyle: The Adventure of the Second Stain

But no chain is stronger than its weakest link.
- Arthur Conan Doyle: The Valley of Fear

Only one important thing has happened in the last three days, and
that is that nothing has happened.
- Arthur Conan Doyle: The Adventure of the Second Stain

I am inclined to think - ' said I. 'I should do so,' Sherlock Holmes remarked impatiently. - Arthur Conan Doyle: The Valley of Fear

I was not surprised when Holmes suggested that I should take my revolver with me. He had himself picked up the loaded hunting-crop, which was his favourite weapon.
- Arthur Conan Doyle: The Adventure of the Six Napoleons

Mediocrity knows nothing higher than itself; but talent instantly
recognizes genius. - Arthur Conan Doyle: The Valley of Fear

I have never been in Africa in my life, so you can put that in your
pipe and smoke it, Mr. Busybody Holmes!
- Arthur Conan Doyle: The Adventure of the Solitary Cyclist

Really, Holmes,' said I severely, 'you are a little trying at times.'
- Arthur Conan Doyle: The Valley of Fear

Made in the USA
Las Vegas, NV
29 November 2024

12856373R00072